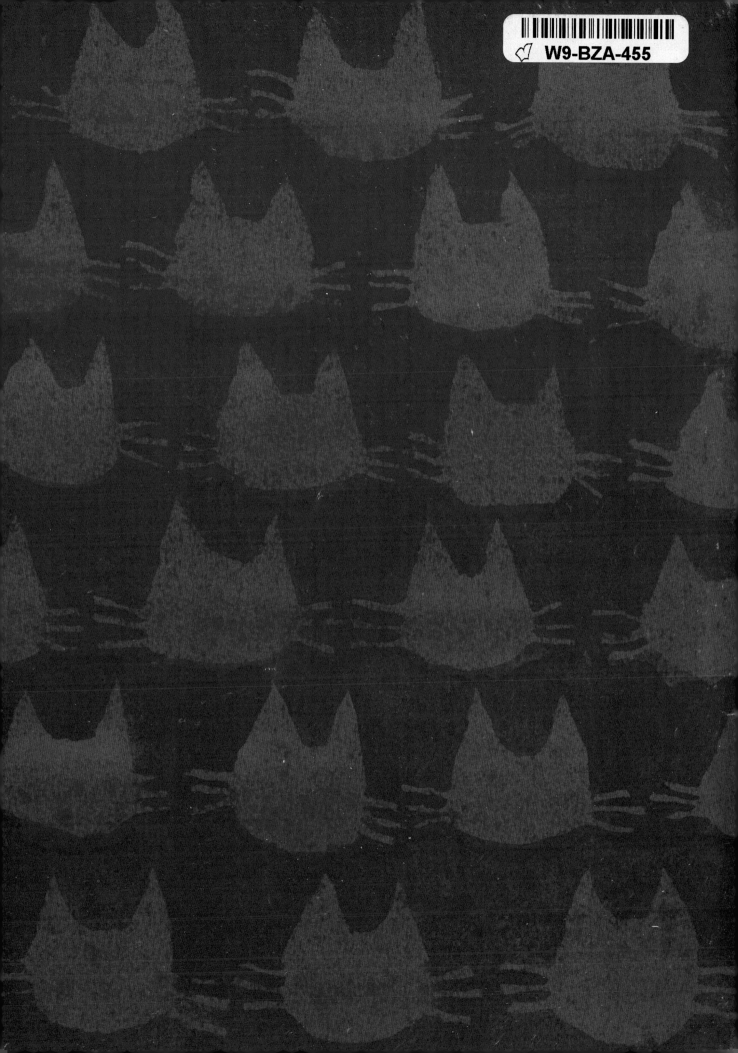

*Late one night an old lady in a pointed hat came in through
my bedroom window. She brandished her broom at me and
fired out some words. Then she left without saying goodbye . . .*

First published in Great Britain by Andersen Press Ltd., 1999
Color separations by Photolitho AG, Zürich
Printed and bound in Italy by Grafiche AZ, Verona
First American edition, 2000

Library of Congress Cataloging-in-Publication Data
Kitamura, Satoshi.
   Me and my cat? / Satoshi Kitamura. — 1st American ed.
      p.   cm.
   Summary: A young boy spends an unusual day after awakening to find
that he and his cat have switched bodies.
   ISBN 0-374-34906-1
   [1. Cats—Fiction.   2. Magic—Fiction.   3. Witches—Fiction.]   I. Title.
PZ7.K6712Me   2000
[E]—dc21   99-16598

Me and My Cat?

SATOSHI KITAMURA

Farrar Straus Giroux
New York

"Nicholas, wake up! You'll be late for school."
It must be Mom. It must be morning again.

Mom dragged me to the bathroom and made me
wash and dress.

Downstairs she interrupted my breakfast.
She was furious.
She carried me off to catch the school bus.
I had gone . . .

but I was still here . . .

"How strange," I thought to myself, pulling my whiskers.

WHISKERS?!

I rushed to the bathroom and looked at myself
in the mirror. Leonardo, my cat, was staring back at me.
But it wasn't him inside. It was me—Nicholas!
I couldn't believe my eyes.
I had turned into a cat!

"Don't panic," I told myself.
I sat in the armchair to consider the situation
carefully . . .
I fell asleep.

When I woke up, I felt a little better.
Maybe it wasn't such a bad thing to be a cat.
I didn't have to go to school, did I?
I hopped onto the table, and from there to the top
of the shelves.
What fun! I could never do *this* before.

I decided to leap toward the cupboard on the other side of
the room. Ready, set . . .

OOPS!

Mom threw me out of the house.

While I was rambling in the garden, Gioconda,
the next-door-neighbor cat, came up and licked me
all over my face.
Yuck!
"Time to go for a walk," I thought.

The brick wall was warm under my paws.
As I got close to Miss Thomson's garden, a funny thought
occurred to me.

Miss Thomson had given me Leonardo when he was
a kitten. Leonardo was Heloise's son.
Did that mean Heloise was now *my* mother?
"Miaow, Miam (Hello, Mom)," I called tentatively.
She ignored me completely.

Farther along, I came across three mean-looking cats.

"Excuse me. May I go through?" I said.

"No, go away! It's our wall," replied one.

"I think the wall belongs to every—"

But before I could finish my sentence
they were all over me.
We punched and kicked and scratched one another
until we fell off the wall, entangled.
"Bowwowowowowowowowow!"
A dog came running toward us, barking furiously.
The cats ran away in all directions.
It was Bernard, Mr. Stone's dog.
He's a sweet dog, my favorite in the neighborhood.

"Thanks, Bernard. You came just in time . . ."
But he chased me out of the garden.
Of course! He couldn't recognize me.

So this was the world that Leonardo lived in.
Life was as tough and complicated as it was for humans.

When I got home, I went into the house. Then I heard
a scratching noise coming from the front door.

It was "me" back from school, trying to get in through
the cat flap.
But was he me, "Nicholas"? Or was he poor little Leonardo
inside my body?

Once indoors, he continued to behave strangely.
He scratched himself earnestly, and when that was done,
he challenged his shoes until they surrendered.

He licked his sweater clean, then spent a long time sharpening his nails.
He found the goldfish particularly fascinating.

He tried to sort the washing, and the yarn . . .
but at last he gave up.

He found the radiator and the litter box irresistible.

But he didn't seem to like *me* at all.

At last, Mom saw something was wrong with her son.
She became so worried that she called the doctor and asked
him to come at once.

"Nothing to worry about," said Dr. Wire. "He's just a little overtired. Send him to bed early and he'll be fine in the morning."

Mom was still very upset. She held him tight in her arms
all evening. I felt sorry for them both.
I climbed on Leonardo-in-my-shape and stroked his cheek.
He purred. Then Mom stroked me gently. I purred.

Later that night, the old lady in the pointed hat came in
through my bedroom window.
"Sorry, love. I got the wrong address," she said.
She brandished her broom and blurted out some words.
Then she left without saying good night.

"Nicholas, wake up! You'll be late for school,"
I heard Mom shouting.
Everything was back to normal.

At school Mr. McGough sat on the table.
He scratched himself, licked his shirt,
and fell asleep for the rest of the lesson.

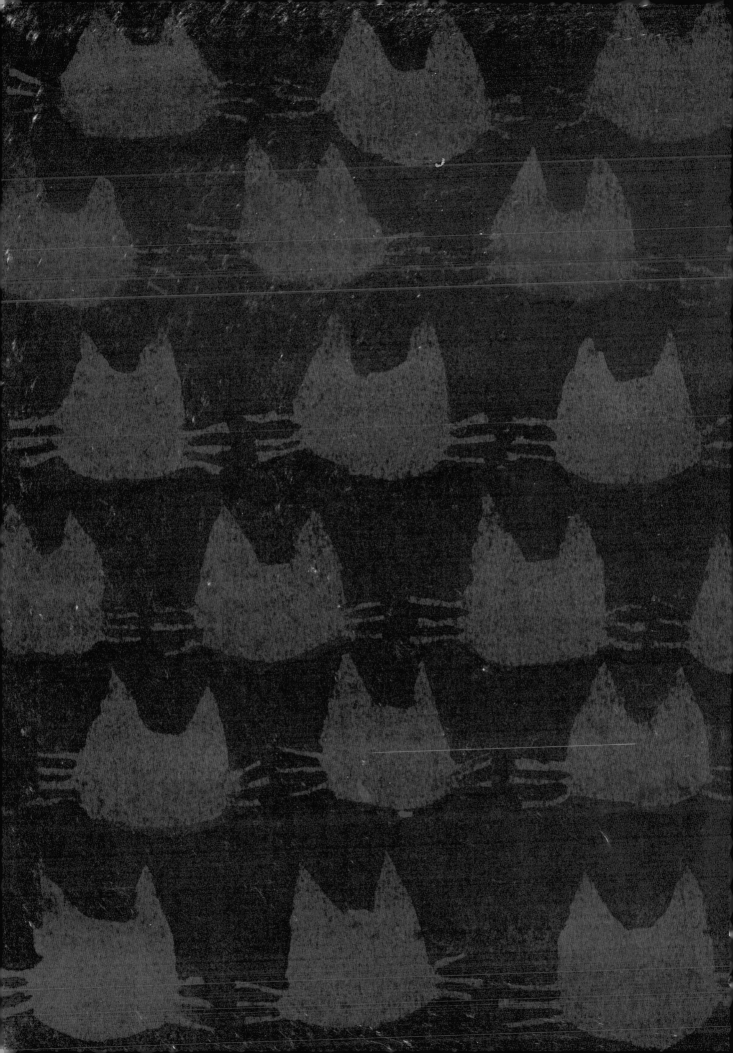